The Big Ideas Club Presents

Young Minds Living Myths

Tragic Cycles

When Lyssa Entered

Untold Oikos Stories

Inside Euripides' Hercules

By Jason Kassel, PhD

Recursive Publishing

Parent Orientation

Reading When Lyssa Entered Together

This book is a retelling of Euripides' tragedy Herakles, one of the most unsettling plays to survive from ancient Greece. It tells the story of a hero who saves his family from destruction, only to lose them afterward when the gods send madness into his home. Euripides wrote this play not to celebrate heroism, but to question it. He asks what happens when strength is asked to carry too much, when gods issue commands without responsibility, and when a family pays the cost of forces far larger than themselves.

When Lyssa Entered is written for families because these questions do not belong only to adults. Children notice when someone they trust changes. They notice when anger, fear, or silence enters a home. They notice when harm happens without clear villains.

This book gives them a language for noticing.

Why Euripides—and Why This Story

Euripides was known, even in his own time, for writing tragedies that unsettled people. His heroes doubt. His gods behave unjustly. His families speak with fear and tenderness instead of certainty.

In Herakles, the children are present onstage, but they are never named. They are loved, protected, and lost—without ever being allowed a voice.

This book gives one of those children a voice.

By telling the story through Deicoon, a child inside the house, the tragedy becomes something families can approach together. The story remains faithful to Euripides' structure and themes, but it is framed through memory, observation, and reflection rather than spectacle.

Nothing is sensationalized. Nothing is erased.

About Lyssa

In Euripides' play, Lyssa is the spirit of madness sent by the gods. She hesitates. She argues. She does not want to enter the house.

This retelling listens closely to that moment.

Lyssa is not presented as a villain, but as a messenger—one who carries out a command she did not choose. Her voice allows children and adults alike to explore a difficult question: What does responsibility look like when harm is ordered, delegated, or passed along?

This is not an excuse for what happens in the story. It is an attempt to understand how tragedy moves through systems, families, and people who are themselves not free.

Structure of the Book

You will notice that this book does not move straight through the tragedy.

Instead, it unfolds in layers:

- scenes   from   inside   the   house

- reflections from children and adults outside the story

- chorus sections that pause and bear witness

- Dinner Table Conversations after each major section

This mirrors how Greek tragedy originally worked. The chorus stopped the action. The audience reflected. Meaning emerged slowly.

The conversations are placed after each story so that families can pause before moving on. You are not expected to read the book all at once.

Reading With Children

Some families will read aloud together. Some will read side by side. Some children will listen quietly and return to the story days later with questions.

All of these responses are appropriate.

You do not need to explain everything. You do not need to protect the story from discomfort. The book is written to hold difficult material with care, and the discussion questions are there to support conversation, not to guide it toward a single conclusion.

What matters most is that the story is shared.

A Final Orientation

Euripides did not write Herakles to tell audiences what to think. He wrote it to make them stop, argue, and remember.

When Lyssa Entered invites families to do the same.

It is a story about a hero who breaks, a family that is lost, and the people who remain afterward—trying to speak, trying to remember, trying to stay.

If this book helps your family talk about anger, fear, responsibility, or love under strain, then it is doing what Euripides intended.

And if the conversation feels unfinished, that is not a failure.

That is tragedy doing its work.

Hercules Son (Deicoon)

A Note to Families and Educators

In Euripides' tragedy Herakles, the children of Herakles are never named. They are present—loved, protected, and tragically lost—but their voices are never heard.

This book gives voice to one of them: Deicoon, a child who loves his father, watches him return, and sees what happens when someone strong carries too much for too long.

By grounding the story in Euripides alone, and telling it through the perspective of a child, this book opens space for families to talk about trauma, grief, and how love does not disappear even when things fall apart.

1: Hero Day at School

We were learning about heroes.

Not the comic kind.

The kind that come home.

Miss Kyria showed us statues—bronze, marble, stone.

Some held shields. Some were missing heads. One had

a lion draped across his back.

"This   is   Herakles,"   she   said.

"He defeated monsters. Saved cities. He was strong.

But when he came home…"

She paused.

Then turned on the screen.

The video was black-and-white. Ancient-sounding.

A courtyard.

A pyre.

A family waiting.

And then—him.

Big, silent. His steps heavy.

He didn't smile.

He didn't wave.

He just looked tired.

I knew that face.

That weight.

That silence.

Because I was there.

I'm Deicoon.

My name isn't in the story they tell. But I was one of the children in the house.

One of the ones who ran to him when he came back.

They say he saved us from the tyrant.

They don't always say what happened next.

The kids in class raised their hands.

"Why doesn't he look happy?"

"Isn't he supposed to be glad to be home?"

"Did he really wear a lion like a coat?"

I didn't raise my hand.

I was just remembering.

I remembered the way he looked at us.

And then—how he didn't.

Miss Kyria stopped the video.

"Herakles suffered something we now call trauma.

He returned from many battles.

But sometimes, when you carry too much for too long...

it breaks inside."

She didn't say what happened to us.

She didn't have to.

2: The Drawing Wall

After the video, Miss Kyria gave us paper.

"Draw what stood out to you," she said.

"What part of the story stayed in your mind?"

Some kids drew the lion skin.

Some drew fire.

One boy drew a huge bow with arrows like spears.

I picked up my pencil and drew a gate.

Not a fancy one.

Just a stone arch. And a shadow walking through it.

I didn't draw his face.

I couldn't yet.

The girl next to me—Sophie—asked:

"Why didn't Herakles smile when he came home?"

I didn't answer.

I was remembering the line from the play, the one Miss Kyria read aloud.

"I would not turn back if I saw all the birds of heaven

flying   against   me."

(Eur. Herakles, line 598)

That's what he said when he came to save us.

Before he even knew what was waiting.

Before the gods sent the thing that broke him.

I   remembered   the   look   on   Grandpa's   face—

Amphitryon—when   Herakles   said   that.

 Like he believed him.

But also… didn't.

Sophie drew wings over her paper.

Black ones.

She didn't know why.

But I did.

I   drew   my   house   next.

Not all of it—just the doorway.

And I made it too small.

Because that's how it felt when he stepped back inside.

Miss Kyria walked behind us, saying nothing. Just nodding.

When she reached mine, she paused.

"Is that the gate of Thebes?" she asked.

I shook my head.

"No,"   I   said.

"It's the part you walk through when you leave something behind."

3: A Father's Shadow

He bent down and lifted me.

His arms were strong. They'd always been strong. But this time, they shook a little.

"You've grown," he said.

His voice was quiet. Not like thunder, like it used to be.

 More like dust settling on stone.

I held on.

Because I had waited.

Because we all had.

My   brothers   ran   to   him.

 Megara stood just behind, her eyes shining—but not with   joy.

 More like fear pretending to be hope.

Grandpa—Amphitryon—stood near the pyre.

He didn't interrupt.

But he was watching.

All of us.

And him.

The people said Herakles had come back just in time.

He had saved us from Lykos, the one who wanted to burn us alive.

But I didn't feel saved.

I felt something else.

When I looked at him, I saw the lion skin across his back.

The   club   resting   on   his   shoulder.

The arrows in his quiver.

But not his eyes.

They weren't resting.

They were... reaching.

He hugged us.

But it felt like he was holding on to a memory.

Like we were already slipping.

Later, Grandpa told him:

"There was a bird above the gate.

A dark one.

Its wings folded wrong."

And Herakles had answered:

"Even if all the birds of heaven flew against me, I

would not turn back."

(Eur. Herakles, 595–598)

He didn't turn back.

He walked into the house.

And we followed.

4: The Wrong Light in His Eyes

It started with the way he looked at Mom.

Not right away.

At first, he smiled—a real one, not big, but the kind

where his eyes soften just a little.

She   smiled   too.

 Tired.

 Worried.

But glad.

Then came the firelight.

We were all gathered—me, my brothers, Mom, Grandpa.

We sat together. We ate. Or tried to.

He didn't touch his food.

He stared at the flames.

"I've seen worse," he said once, almost to himself.

 "Worse than this. Much worse."

Mom reached across the table.

"You're home now."

He   blinked.

 Nodded.

But his shoulders didn't settle.

Grandpa said something—I don't remember what.

Maybe it was about the gods.

Maybe it was about rest.

But then... he stood up.

He looked at me.

At my brothers.

At Mom.

But the light in his eyes wasn't soft anymore.

It was sharp.

Not angry.

Just... scared.

But not of us.

Of something else.

Something we couldn't see.

He took a step back.

Then forward.

Then grabbed his bow.

Mom stood.

"It's   us,"   she   said.

 "It's your family."

He didn't hear her.

Or maybe he did.

But not with the part of himself that knew what "family" meant.

His eyes looked the same way the fire did.

5: When the Wind Changed

It   happened   all   at   once.

And not all at once.

Like a storm you didn't see until the sky was already

broken.

The   wind   came   through   the   courtyard.

Not   loud.   Not   cold.

But wrong.

The kind of wind that doesn't carry leaves.

It carries voices.

"Drive   him,"   one   of   them   said.

"Twist the heart of the strongest one."

I didn't see her.

But I felt her.

Grandpa said it later.

He said the gods sent someone called Lyssa—the spirit of madness.

She   didn't   throw   anything.

 She didn't scream.

She just pushed him from the inside.

And   then   my   father—

 the man who held up the sky in stories—

looked at me like I was something else.

"Monster," he said.

Not loud.

But enough.

Mom stepped in front of me.

"No. No—he's your son."

But the fire in his eyes didn't cool.

The bow was still in his hand.

The club still by his feet.

My brothers were crying.

I don't know when I started.

Maybe I didn't.

Maybe I just watched.

Watched the hands that used to carry us—

tighten.

[Back at the school – CHILD CHORUS]

A student drops her pencil.

No one speaks.

Then one voice—soft:

"Sometimes people don't mean to hurt the ones they

love."

Another:

"But they do anyway."

Miss Kyria turns off the projector.

The class is quiet.

No one draws anymore.

Just one boy, in the back, holding his picture of a father with the sky behind him—

but no face.

6: The House That Fell Without a Sound

I don't remember the scream.

I don't remember the crash.

I don't remember which hand held the bow.

I just remember the sky.

Gray.

Not stormy.

Just still.

They say I died quickly.

That I didn't see it coming.

That I didn't know.

But I did.

Not all of it.

But enough.

I saw his eyes.

I saw Mom reach for me.

I saw the light shift in the courtyard.

And then—

nothing.

No pain.

Just a small thought.

"I hope he remembers me."

[Back at the school – CHILD CHORUS]

Sophie raises her hand.

"What happened to the kids?"

Miss Kyria pauses.

Her voice is kind. But sure.

"They   were   taken   too   early.

Not   by   choice.   Not   by   hate.

But by something broken inside someone who loved

them."

Kalem, the quiet boy, whispers:

"Like when a bridge falls, even if you built it strong."

No one laughs.

No one moves.

Only one hand begins drawing again.

This   time,   a   house—not   a   big   one.

Not   burning.

Just... quiet.

A small figure stands outside.

Waiting.

Watching.

Holding something in his hand.

7: What He Carried

He didn't run.

He didn't shout.

He didn't hide.

He knelt in the courtyard.

Among the ashes.

Among the silence.

Among everything he could never put back.

Grandpa told me later:

"He tried to take his own life."

But Theseus stopped him.

Not   with   a   sword.

 Not with a shield.

With words.

With friendship.

With a promise:

"Come with me. I'll take you to Athens."

I think he didn't say yes right away.

Because the part of him that had carried so much—

didn't know how to carry this.

Not monsters.

Not labors.

Not gods.

But what he had done.

He held his bow one last time.

Then let it fall.

He looked at Mom.

At where we had been.

And maybe—

just for a second—

he saw us again.

I hope he did.

[Back at the school – CHILD CHORUS]

Miss Kyria asks:

"What do we do with stories like this? When the hero breaks?"

A hand goes up.

"We tell them anyway."

Another:

"So we remember what love looks like—even when it's broken."

8: When I Am Big

When I am big, I will remember.

Not just the way he fell.

But the way he carried us—
before the silence.
Before the fire.

When I am big, I will know that strength isn't always
a roar.
Sometimes it's a whisper.
A hand on your shoulder.
A father trying, even when he can't finish the
sentence.

When I am big, I won't forget that people break.
Even heroes.
Even dads.
Even me.

But I'll also remember this:

He came back.

He stood between us and the fire.

He tried to hold us.

He tried.

And   maybe   that's   what   love   is—

not   always   perfect,

not   always   enough,

but still real.

[Back at the school – ADULT CHORUS ENTERS]

Miss Kyria collects the drawings.

Parents wait by the door.

Grandpa sits in the hallway, his cane by his side.

A few teachers wipe their eyes, quietly.

The students hang their pictures on the wall—

a house, a gate, a lion skin, a club left behind.

One parent kneels beside their child and asks:

"Was it a sad story?"

The child nods.

"But not only sad."

Another child adds:

"It's a remembering story."

When I am big, I will remember.

Family Discussion Questions

1. Why do you think Herakles didn't smile when he came home?

   o What did you notice about how he changed?

2. What does Deicoon remember most about his father?

   o What do you think is the most important thing to remember about someone you love?

3. Have you ever seen someone be strong even when they were hurting inside?

- How can we help each other when we don't always understand what's wrong?

4. What does it mean to say this is a "remembering story"?

   - Why is it important to tell stories, even when they're sad?

Glossary

- Herakles – A famous hero in Greek mythology, known for completing twelve impossible labors. In this story, he returns from battle changed.
- Oikos – A Greek word meaning household or home. It includes the people, the place, and the memory of both.
- Trauma – A deep hurt that stays inside someone, often caused by something frightening, painful, or overwhelming.

- Lyssa – In Greek mythology, the spirit of madness and unreason. In Herakles, she is sent by the gods to break him.
- Philos – A word that means deep friendship and loyal love—especially in the hardest times.

Lyssa

Prologue: Before the Command

My name is Lyssa.

In your tongue, it means rage.

But that's not what I am.

In my first breath, they named me for a wolf.

In my second, they taught me to bite.

In my third, they told me: Go.

I didn't want to.

I never want to.

But I am the one the gods send

when no one else will carry what must be done.

I am not punishment.

I am not choice.

I am the shadow that follows silence.

My name comes from λύω—

It means to loosen,

to unbind,

to break apart.

They tied it to wolves—

λύκος—because wolves take what no one defends.

So I became all three:

Lyssa, who enters.

Lykos, who devours.

The Wolf, who watches the house fall.

But I did not want to come.

I am not Herakles' enemy.

I was sent.

I warned them.

I begged them.

But the gods whispered back:

"He must break."

Chapter 1: I Wait at the Gate

She was angry.

Not at me.

 Not even at the boy in the house.

But at the one above.

The one who took what he wanted.

 The one who broke what he touched.

And never stopped to ask if it could be made whole again.

She couldn't reach him.

So she reached sideways.

Downward.

To the house of his child.

And she sent me.

I stood at the edge of the gate.

Not   out   of   fear.

But out of sorrow.

Inside,   there   was   a   mother.

A   father.

Sleeping   children.

A man just home from long suffering.

He   had   fought   monsters.

Crossed   oceans.

Bent the world back into shape.

And now?

He   smiled.

He   took   off   his   lion   skin.

He set down his bow.

I didn't want to enter.

I said it clearly:

"This   house   is   full   of   love."

"Why must I bring fire to what is already fragile?"

But no one answered.

Not the queen who sent me.

Not the gods who watched.

Only silence.

So I waited.

I waited at the gate.

Longer than they wanted me to.

Because sometimes the only thing you can do

when you're sent to break—

is to hesitate.

Chapter 2: I Was Not Made for This

I was made.

Not born.

Not chosen.

Just shaped—by the hands of gods who needed someone to carry their worst commands.

They didn't give me laughter.

They didn't give me dreams.

They   gave   me   one   thing:

"Enter where it hurts."

I asked once—

"Why me?"

They said—

"Because you do not flinch."

But they were wrong.

I do.

Every time.

I was not made for love.

I was not made for songs.

I was not made to save.

I   was   made   to   step   across   the   line

between   what   could   have   been

and what now cannot be undone.

And yet—

I   still   feel   sorrow

for every house I enter.

Every voice I silence.

Every story I scatter.

I am not the storm.

I am the one who carries it in.

So I stayed at the gate.

Longer than they wanted.

Watching the family inside.

Seeing   what   would   be   lost—

and who would be blamed.

Because when the gods send pain,

they   never   say

"We did this."

They send me.

And then walk away.

Chapter 3: They Told Me Where to Strike

I asked—

"Why   him?"

"Hasn't   he   suffered   enough?"

"Didn't he finish every labor you set?"

They said:

"Yes."

But then they said—

"He   is   too   proud."

"He   thinks   he's   free."

"Strike him where it will humble him."

So I asked—

"His   strength?"

"His name?"

And they said:

"No."

"Strike   him   in   his   love."

"Strike   the   part   that   ties   him   to   others."

"Unmake his home."

I flinched.

Even I.

I said:

"If I enter that house, the whole world will shake."

But they didn't answer.

They just opened the door.

I   had   no   sword.

No   thunder.

No roar.

Only silence, and the key they handed me.

So I stepped forward.

I   did   not   break   the   wall.

I only touched the heart.

And he broke himself.

Because that is how it works.

The worst tragedies come not from anger—

But from being used.

[INTERLUDE – MODERN CHILD CHORUS]

Nico:

"She didn't want to hurt him."

Sara:

"She just followed orders."

Amina:

"They told her where it would hurt most."

Devon:

"And she still asked them not to."

Chapter 4: I Touched the Hero

I did not roar.

I did not scream.

I did not throw him into fire.

I simply touched him.

Softly.

Not   his   arm.

 Not his head.

His love.

That's where they told me to go.

The   part   that   held   him   together.

The part that belonged to his family, not to the gods.

He was smiling.

His children laughed.

His wife leaned against the doorway.

And I thought—

"If I do this, they will never be the same."

Then I remembered—

"That's what they want."

So I reached forward.

And I loosened the knot inside his heart.

Just enough.

He blinked.

Twice.

Then the light in his eyes changed.

He   stood.

He   looked.

But not at them.

He saw something else.

Something far away.

Something wrong.

And the worst part?

He believed it.

I never touched the children.

I never touched the wife.

But I took him away from them.

And that was enough.

[INTERLUDE – MODERN CHILD CHORUS]

Amina:

"She didn't break the house."

Devon:

"She broke the part that held it together."

Nico:

"She touched love. That's what they told her to do."

Sara:

"And she cried, even though no one saw it."

Chapter 5: I Vanish Before the Fire

I did not stay.

That's not what I'm made to do.

They don't want me to see what follows.

They   want   me   to   start   the   ruin—

not carry its weight.

So   after   I   touched   the   hero,

after   the   knot   of   love   came   loose,

after the light left his eyes—

I stepped backward.

One breath.

And I was gone.

The gods prefer it that way.

No footprints.

No sound.

Only questions.

"What	happened		to	him?"
"Why	did	he	do	that?"
"How		could		he—?"
"Why would a father—?"				

They don't answer.

Because they didn't hold the bow.

But I know what they did.

And I know what I did.

I saw the fire begin in the eyes of the children.

 Not from the torch.

From the confusion.

The silence.

The love they lost before they could name it.

And I wept.

Not out loud.

But the kind of weeping only spirits do—

the kind the gods ignore.

[INTERLUDE – MODERN CHILD CHORUS]

Devon:

"She didn't run."

Nico:

"She vanished."

Sara:

"So no one could blame her."

Amina:

"But she blamed herself anyway."

They blamed the man who carried the madness.

They mourned the family.

But no one remembered the one who opened the gate.

Chapter 6: I Am Not the End

They call me a spirit of rage.

They say I bring madness.

They teach that when I enter, everything ends.

But that isn't true.

I   am   not   the   fire.

I   am   the   hand   that   lights   the   match—

because someone else left it waiting.

I come when no one else wants to take responsibility.

When   the   gods   stay   silent.

When   the   leaders   look   away.

When the pain grows so big, it has to go somewhere.

So they send me.

But I am not the end.

The end comes later.

In the quiet.

In the faces that no longer recognize each other.

In the voices that go still because they've run out of

things to lose.

I am not hate.

I am not cruelty.

I am the messenger.

And I did not want to come.

But I did.

And now, I leave.

And   if   you   remember   me—

not   as   the   fury,

not   as   the   destroyer,

but as the one who tried to stop at the gate—

then maybe the next time someone is breaking,

you   will   not   ask,

"What's wrong with them?"

You will ask,

"Who sent the storm?"

[FINAL PANEL – MODERN CHILD CHORUS]

Sara:

"She was a warning."

Devon:

"She didn't choose this."

Amina:

"She said no. And they made her go anyway."

Nico (quietly):

"We won't forget her."

A Note to Readers and Families

Lyssa is not a villain.

In the ancient play Herakles, she is sent by the gods to cause madness. But in this retelling, we listen to her voice.

She doesn't want to go.

She doesn't hate the people in the house.

She simply carries what others won't—the orders, the silence, and the storm.

This book helps children understand what it means to feel powerless in the face of large, confusing forces—and how speaking about it can be an act of courage.

Discussion Questions

1. Why didn't Lyssa want to go into the house?

- What did she see there that made her hesitate?

2. Why do the gods send her, but never take responsibility?

   - Have you ever seen someone get blamed for something they didn't choose?

3. What does Lyssa mean when she says, "I was not the end"?

   - Who or what do you think actually caused the pain?

4. What are some kinds of storms people carry today?

   - How can we help others without making them feel broken?

5. Can someone be part of something bad without being a bad person?

   - How do we talk about responsibility when it's shared or hidden?

Glossary

- Lyssa – In ancient Greek, her name means "rage" or "madness." In this story, she is a reluctant messenger who brings harm she doesn't want to cause.

- Lykos – A tyrant in the Herakles play. His name means "wolf." He, Lyssa, and the image of the wolf all represent destructive forces unleashed by power.

- PTSD (Post-Traumatic Stress Disorder) – A strong emotional injury caused by terrifying or overwhelming events. It doesn't mean someone is weak. It means they've carried too much.

- Messenger – Someone who brings a message or carries out a command. In myths, messengers often speak truth that others are afraid to say.

- Oikos – A Greek word for household, family, and all the bonds that make a home. When the oikos falls, it's not just walls that break—it's trust, memory, and love.

A Final Thought

Some   stories   are   hard.
Some   messengers   don't   get   to   choose.
Some children grow up asking why no one stopped the fire.

This   book   says:
  Maybe   someone   tried.
  Maybe it was Lyssa.
And   maybe   now,
  it's your turn to speak.

Chorus

Chapter 1: The Hall of Echoes

It was a quiet room.

Low   ceiling.

Coffee   urns   humming   in   the   corner.

Photos in faded frames on the wall—some of them
were younger versions of the men now seated.

No   music   played.

Only   the   sound   of   folding   chairs.

And the weight of memory.

CHORUS MEMBER 1 (softly):

"We sang for him. You remember?"

CHORUS MEMBER 2:

"Louder than anyone else. Before the fall."

CHORUS MEMBER 3:

"But not when it counted."

They didn't look at each other when they said it.

It was enough to speak.

CHORUS MEMBER 1:

"We knew the house was cracking.

Knew the boy was out too long.

Knew the fire was lit at the edge of the wall."

CHORUS MEMBER 2:

"But we waited."

CHORUS MEMBER 3:

"We watched."

CHORUS MEMBER 1:

"And then we said, 'Let us go.'"

One of them unfolded an old program.

It still said Oikos – Saved by Herakles at the top.

He let it fall onto the table.

CHORUS MEMBER 2:

"We weren't just witnesses."

CHORUS MEMBER 3:

"We were the chorus of a broken polis."

They sat in silence again.

Not out of honor.

Out of shame.

Out of the strange knowledge that singing the tragedy

isn't the same as preventing it.

Chapter 2: Swan Song

The lights buzzed above.

No one reached for the microphone.

This wasn't that kind of meeting.

CHORUS MEMBER 1 took a sip of cold coffee.

Then spoke—not to the room, but to the table.

"I   remember   saying:

'Even the gods watch Herakles with pride.'"

He shook his head.

"But   they   didn't.

 And we said it anyway."

CHORUS MEMBER 2 leaned forward.

"I   said:

 'Let Thebes rejoice, for the oikos stands tall!'"

"It was already burning when I sang that line."

CHORUS MEMBER 3, the oldest among them, opened

a folder—full of typed scripts, paperclipped notes.

He found one.

He read aloud:

"The bow unstrung rests on the stone / The house is

safe, the labors done."

He paused.

Folded the paper.

"We   thought   it   was   a   poem.

 It was an obituary."

Silence.

Then CHORUS MEMBER 1 again:

"Do you remember the last thing we said?"

No one answered.

He said it for them.

'Let us go.'

The words hung in the room like smoke.

CHORUS MEMBER 2:

"We said it so gently."

CHORUS MEMBER 3:

"As if that made it less of a betrayal."

CHORUS MEMBER 1 looked up for the first time.

"We   were   the   chorus.

 We should have stayed."

Chapter 3: What We Saw But Didn't Say

The rain had started outside.

Just a whisper against the windows.

Inside, the men sat beneath ceiling fans that didn't turn.

They didn't look at each other when they spoke.

Only at the table.

CHORUS MEMBER 3 tapped a folded program with two fingers.

"I saw the children at the window. One had a stick, pretending it was a bow. The other one said, 'Do you think he'll know us?'"

He closed his eyes.

"I sang over that. I chose metaphor."

CHORUS MEMBER 2 leaned back, staring at the ceiling tiles.

"When Lykos entered the courtyard,
I felt the old fight in my hands.
I had stood at the wall once.
I had held a spear once."

"But I said, 'Let the gods decide.'"

CHORUS MEMBER 1 folded his hands.

"I watched Amphitryon bow his head—not in shame,
but because the city had already disappeared."

"I wanted to stand beside him.
But we were the chorus."

"And I thought... that was enough."

They sat in silence again.

Not because there was nothing left to say.

But because saying nothing had once been their role—

and they were trying to unlearn it.

CHORUS MEMBER 2:

"We didn't fail to see."

CHORUS MEMBER 3:

"We failed to stand."

Chapter 4: If We Had Stayed

No one said they could have stopped the madness.

No one claimed they would've changed the gods' will.

But sitting there—shoulders curved, hands still strong in places—they began to imagine something quieter than heroics.

Something smaller than salvation.

CHORUS MEMBER 1:

"If we had stayed, he wouldn't have buried them alone."

CHORUS MEMBER 2:

"Amphitryon wouldn't have had to speak into empty air.

He would've had someone to hear him."

CHORUS MEMBER 3:

"We   could've   stood   in   the   doorway.

Just   stood.

So the tyrant wouldn't have seen a house without

men."

The fan clicked on above them—slow, halting.

One of them smiled faintly.

"No   music.

Just   our   boots   on   the   stones.

Our breath in the silence."

CHORUS MEMBER 2:

"We always thought we were too old. Too tired. Too

lyrical."

CHORUS MEMBER 1:

"But sometimes showing up is louder than any line we ever sang."

They didn't rewrite the ending.

They just imagined a different kind of exit.

Not "Let us go."

But—

"We're still here."

Chapter 5: The Song We Never Sang

They didn't stand.

They didn't face an audience.

They just sat together in the VFW hall, chairs creaking under memory.

And they spoke—together, not in unison, but in harmony.

"To Amphitryon," they said.

"You   were   the   one   who   stayed.
When   we   sang   of   strength,
it was your silence that held the house."

"You   stood   while   the   tyrant   spoke.
You   stood   when   no   god   answered.
You stood while the city disappeared behind you."

"And when your son broke beneath the weight of
what   he   carried,
you   did   not   curse   him.
You   did   not   run.
You simply watched. And bore it."

"We should have stood beside you."
"We should have seen that the oikos is not a myth.
It is a man, holding a line, with no one left to guard
his back."

"You were the last citizen.

The last fighter.

The last father."

One of them raised a cup of cold coffee.

The others followed.

And they all said together—

"We remember you."

"We're sorry we left."

"We won't forget again."

A Note to Readers and Educators

In most Greek tragedies, the chorus watches. They sing. They narrate. But they do not intervene.

In Herakles, the chorus speaks beautifully—until the house falls.

Then they say: "Let us go."

This book is their answer to that line.

What happens when witnesses realize they abandoned what they were meant to protect?

What does it mean to sing after it's too late?

In this retelling, the chorus returns—not to undo, but to remember. They don't rewrite the ending. They stay.

Discussion Questions

1. What did the chorus mean by "Let us go"?

    o Why do you think Euripides gave them that as their final line?

2. Why did the chorus come back in this book?

    o What were they trying to do, or undo?

3. Do you think they were responsible for what happened?

    o What does responsibility mean when you're not the one holding the sword?

4. Have you ever been a witness to something hard?

○ How can people act with courage even if
 they can't fix everything?

5. What does it mean to say: "We remember you.
 We won't forget again"?

 ○ Who in your life deserves to be
 remembered like that?

Glossary

- Chorus – In Greek tragedy, a group who
 comments on the action. In this story, they
 become the voice of the city—and its regret.

- Oikos – A Greek word meaning household,
 home, family—and all it stands for.

- Katastrophē – A tragic turning point or collapse.
 Often, it comes not from one action, but from
 many small silences.

- Witness – Someone who sees. Sometimes,
 witnessing is a moral act. Sometimes, it is not
 enough.

- Swan Song – A final, beautiful expression before death or departure. In tragedy, it can be both sorrowful and true.

Theseus

Chapter 1: The Place Without Light

Before the ruin of the house. Before the fall. There was

darkness. Endless, echoing darkness.

THESEUS (narrating)

I was there.

Not in a prison.

 Not in a storm.

But in a place where time stopped speaking.

They call it Hades.

But I remember it only as stillness.

No sky.

 No footsteps.

 No seasons.

Just silence.

And the weight of what I could never undo.

I   had   gone   too   far.

Reached   too   high.

Tried to take something that didn't belong to me.

And so—I fell.

Down into the place without light.

No one came.

Not   for   months.

Not for years.

Maybe not ever.

Then—

one sound.

A step.

Then another.

Not   a   god.

 Not a ghost.

Herakles.

He saw me, bound in the stone.

He didn't ask how I got there.

He didn't ask if I deserved it.

He just reached down and said—

"You don't belong here."

And he pulled me out.

Back   into   the   air.

 Back   into   time.

 Back into the world.

THESEUS (present)

That was the day I learned what philos means.

It means—

"I   know   what   the   darkness   is   like,

and I won't let you stay there alone."

Chapter 1: The Place Without Light

Two   boys   sit   outside   the   principal's   office.

They   don't   talk.

They   don't   look   at   each   other.

Their shoes don't touch.

They were best friends.

Until yesterday.

Now?

Now they just wait.

The   wall   clock   clicks.

 The secretary types.

No one calls their name.

One of them, the taller one, rubs the back of his hand.

"He didn't have to say that."

He   doesn't   say   it   out   loud.

 Just inside.

Where the ache is sharper than the words.

Then something strange happens.

He remembers a story.

One they read together.

Before the fight.

Before everything got weird.

The story begins again—not in school, but in a place without sky.

THESEUS (narrating)

I was there.

In the Underworld.

Not   dreaming.

 Not   asleep.

 Just... forgotten.

They call it Hades.

But I called it quiet.

So quiet it felt like the world had stopped breathing.

I don't remember how long I was there.

Time is slower where sorrow lives.

Then I heard it.

A step.

Then another.

Not   a   ghost.

 Not a judge.

Herakles.

He   didn't   ask   what   I'd   done.

 He didn't ask why I'd fallen.

He just reached.

"You don't belong here," he said.

And he pulled me out.

That's when I knew what philos meant.

Not just "friend."

"Someone who remembers you when the world forgets."

Back outside the principal's office, the two boys still sit apart.

But the shorter one glances sideways.

 Just for a second.

Not a smile.

 Not yet.

But maybe something like remembering.

Chapter 2: The Ashes of a Friend

Thebes is quiet.

No bells. No horns. No voices from the gates.

Just a door left half-open, and no one willing to cross its threshold.

Theseus walks inside.

The house does not smell of fire.

But everything feels burned.

No children.

No wife.

Only an old man standing in the shadows.

Only Herakles, sitting on the stones.

He doesn't lift his head.

He doesn't look up.

He just whispers—

"I did this."

Theseus does not ask how.

Does not ask why.

He already knows.

THESEUS

The gods sent you to save the world.

But they didn't save you.

HERAKLES

Don't stay here.

I'm not worth your shadow.

THESEUS

You came for me in a place no one visits.

Now I am here.

Herakles turns, just slightly.

His eyes are red.

But Theseus doesn't flinch.

He sits beside him.

They don't speak for a long time.

But they don't need to.

CHORUS OF OLD MEN (softly)

He came.

Not   with   sword.

 Not with shield.

But with presence.

And that is more than the gods have done.

Back outside the principal's office...

The taller boy shifts.

His foot moves a little closer to the other's.

They still don't speak.

But the distance is changing.

Chapter 3: No One Fixes This

Herakles   sits   in   the   rubble.

His   hands   are   quiet   now.

His strength has nowhere left to go.

HERAKLES

You shouldn't see me like this.

You shouldn't have come.

THESEUS

I didn't come to see a hero.

I came because you're my friend.

Herakles looks away.

"I   lost   everything,"   he   says.

"They sent me to protect the world. And I destroyed

my own house."

Theseus doesn't answer right away.

He listens.

Not   because   he   has   an   answer—

but because someone finally needs to hear it.

THESEUS

I won't fix this.

No one can.

Herakles breathes.

Once.

 Then again.

"Then why stay?" he asks.

THESEUS

Because philos means—

I   carry   a   piece   of   your   pain,

 so you don't have to carry all of it alone.

The two of them sit in the ash.

They say nothing else for a while.

And that's okay.

CHORUS OF OLD MEN

We thought strength meant swinging the club.

We thought friendship meant glory in battle.

But this—

This is the only thing that's still standing.

Back outside the principal's office...

The shorter boy slides a note across the bench.

 It says just two words:

"You okay?"

Chapter 4: The Rope, Not the Ladder

The sun begins to set on the ruined house.

 There are no flames now. Just dust, and the ache of

what's gone.

Herakles rests his head in his hands.

"I don't deserve to walk out of here."

Theseus doesn't argue.

He doesn't disagree.

He just says:

"Then I'll sit here with you."

"For how long?" Herakles asks.

"As long as it takes."

There's no victory speech.

No god descends with golden light.

No undoing of what was done.

But Theseus stays.

And that changes everything.

THESEUS

I'm   not   a   ladder   to   fix   you.

 I'm a rope.

I   won't   lift   you   unless   you   reach.

 But I won't leave you swinging.

Herakles finally stands.

Not   proud.

 Not strong.

But standing.

And he asks:

"Where would I go?"

Theseus says:

"Where I go."

CHORUS OF OLD MEN

The   house   has   fallen.

 The city watched.

But   one   friend   came   through   the   gate.

 And he did not flinch.

Back outside the principal's office...

The taller boy writes back.

"I'm not okay. But thanks."

The shorter one nods.

The   distance   between   them—

is almost gone.

Chapter 5: The Walk Away

Morning light touches the stones of the house. Herakles stands in the doorway. The club is still. The bow left behind.

HERAKLES

I said I would return to bury him.

But I won't.

THESEUS

He knows that.

HERAKLES

He   raised   me.

He   stood   at   the   wall.

He watched the gods abandon us.

And now I leave him.

THESEUS

He stayed, so you could go.

He gave you what no god would:

A place to start from.

Herakles turns back once. Amphitryon stands silently

in the courtyard.

No words pass between them.

But Herakles places his hand over his heart.

And walks away.

CHORUS OF OLD MEN

O Amphitryon—

You are the last piece of the house.

Not   a   ruin.

Not   a   warning.

A witness.

Your   son   walks   toward   something   new.

Not   with   triumph.

With a friend.

And that is more than most.

Amphitryon   does   not   speak.

But he lifts his head.

Back outside the principal's office...

The door creaks open.

The principal calls them in.

But before they go, the taller boy says—

"I'm sorry."

The shorter boy nods.

"Me too."

And they walk in—together.

Chapter 6: The Thread That Holds

The road out of Thebes is quiet.
There is no parade. No celebration.
Just two figures walking side by side.

CHORUS OF OLD MEN

He could not carry the grief alone.
So a friend came.
And took one corner of the weight.

Not to fix.
Not to judge.
Just to stay.

And that thread—
invisible, unbreakable—
is called philos.

HERAKLES

I am not whole.

THESEUS

Then we walk.

Not toward answers.

Just forward.

And they do.

No   crown.

 No   song.

Just   the   sound   of   two   sets   of   footsteps

on a road long enough to carry sorrow.

Back at school...

The two boys leave the principal's office.

They don't say much.

But one of them holds the door.

And the other waits.

They walk down the hall.

Not   as   enemies.

 Not as strangers.

As friends again.

Even   when   it   hurts.

 Even when it's not easy.

That's what friends do.

A Note to Readers and Families

This story is not about saving the day.

It's about what happens after.

When   everything   is   broken.

 When   no   one   knows   what   to   say.

 When the hero has fallen—and the gods are silent.

That's when philos appears.

Not   loud.

Not   with   answers.

Just present.

This book tells how a friend—Theseus—entered the

ashes   and   stayed.

Not   to   fix   Herakles.

Just to carry what he could.

And maybe to help him walk again.

Discussion Questions

1. What did Theseus do that the gods and city did
   not?

   o Why is that more powerful than thunder or
     fire?

2. Herakles didn't ask for help—but Theseus came
   anyway.

   o When is it okay to just show up for
     someone?

3. What's the difference between a hero and a friend?

    o Which is harder to be?

4. Have you ever had a fight with a close friend?

    o What helped you repair the friendship?

5. What does it mean to be a "rope, not a ladder," like Theseus?

    o How can that idea help in real life?

Glossary

- Philos – An ancient Greek word for deep friendship. Not just liking someone. Loving them enough to walk through hard things with them.

- Herakles – A hero who carried more than anyone. But not even he could carry grief alone.

- Theseus – A king who had once been saved. And who came back—not to repay, but to remain.

- Amphitryon – Herakles' father. He stands in silence, proud and broken. He represents the pain of letting someone grow away.

- Chorus – The old men of Thebes who witness everything. They speak when no one else will.

- Thread – What ties two people together, even when things fall apart.

A Final Thought

You don't need to be the strongest person in the room.

You just need to stay.

And when someone is sitting in silence—

you don't need to fix them.

You just need to sit beside them.

That's philos.

That's enough.

The Tragedy of Hercules' Madness

Chapter 1: The Gate Is Closed

A courtyard. The stones are cracked. The sky is silent.

An old man speaks.

AMPHITRYON

My   name   is   Amphitryon.

I was once known as a man of Thebes.

Now   I   am   only   a   father,

waiting   at   a   closed   gate,

guarding children I cannot protect.

They sent my son—Herakles—to fight monsters.

Twelve   labors.

Twelve trials.

He   never   said   no.

Not   to   kings.

Not to gods.

And   now   that   he's   gone,

the city pretends he was never here.

There   are   no   guards   at   my   side.

No   friends.

No shield-bearers.

Only   silence.

And the man outside the wall who wants to burn

what's left.

His   name   is   Lykos.

He calls himself king.

But he rules only by fear.

He wants to destroy this house so no one remembers

the name Herakles.

Let him try.

I will not kneel.

Enter the CHORUS of OLD MEN of Thebes.

CHORUS

O   house   of   strength,

once   loud   with   the   footsteps   of   a   hero—

now quiet.

We   are   too   old   to   stand   at   the   wall.

Our   swords   have   rusted.

Our knees bend in pain.

But still—we come.

Not   with   weapons.

But   with   eyes   that   see

what the city no longer wants to see:

The   children   inside.

The   fire   outside.

The silence above.

O   Thebes—

have you forgotten?

The   hands   that   once   held   back   disaster

now tremble behind closed doors.

And still no one answers.

Amphitryon stands silent, facing the gate.

CHORUS

Will no one come?

Will no god lift a finger?

Let us wait with the father.

Let us witness what may fall.

Even if we cannot hold it up.

Chapter 2: The Wall That Speaks

The courtyard. The door is barred. Inside stand Megara, her children, and Amphitryon. Outside, the tyrant Lykos calls out.

LYKOS (from outside)

Open the door.

Herakles   is   gone.

 His name means nothing now.

You're   not   a   queen   anymore.

 You're the last problem in a house I plan to erase.

MEGARA (calmly)

You want me to beg?

You won't get it.

You bring a torch to a home already wounded.

 You call it strength to threaten children?

LYKOS

I offer you mercy.

Bow your head and I'll spare the little ones.
Maybe even you.

MEGARA

If I teach my children to survive by begging,
they'll forget who their father was.
I would rather they fall as Herakles' sons—
than live as your shadows.

Lykos does not reply. He lifts the torch.

CHORUS

O woman of iron,
you do not tremble.
You speak as one who has already seen the worst—
and still stands.

Your voice is a wall no fire can cross.

Yet what can we do?

Our   hands   are   slow.

Our backs bent.

We   stand   and   speak,

but speech does not turn back a tyrant.

Thebes has grown quiet.

Too quiet to save her own.

Inside, Megara turns to Amphitryon.

MEGARA

He will break the door.

He will light the pyre.

You   cannot   stop   him,

and I will not kneel.

So we stand.

Together.

Until the fire comes.

CHORUS

O gods, do you see?

O Zeus, do you care?

You send Herakles to clean the world—

but who guards the ones he left behind?

Chapter 3: The Hero Returns Too Late

The pyre has been built. Lykos lifts his torch. The house stands quiet. Then—

HERAKLES (offstage)

Put it down.

Lykos freezes. The torch wavers. The gate swings open. Herakles steps into the courtyard.

HERAKLES

Put it down now.

Or I will.

LYKOS (startled)

You—

You   were   gone.

  You were supposed to be far from here.

HERAKLES

I was.

Now I am here.

And you are standing on the threshold of my house

  with   a   torch   in   your   hand

  and threats in your mouth.

LYKOS (drawing his weapon)

You are too late.

This house was already falling.

HERAKLES (raising his club)

Then let me decide what still stands.

The fight is swift. The club falls. Lykos does not rise.

Herakles turns to see his children, Megara, Amphitryon. The pyre still smolders. No one cheers.

HERAKLES

I thought I would return to joy.

I thought I would walk in and hear my children's laughter.

But this is not joy.

MEGARA (quietly)

You came.

But the fire was already here.

CHORUS

O   heart   that   hoped,

 now trembling.

We sang that Herakles would come in time.

And he did.

But time plays cruel tricks.

Even heroes arrive late.

You   held   the   club.

 You stopped the tyrant.

But   the   fire   in   your   house—

it already burns low.

HERAKLES (to Megara)

Forgive me.

For being far.

For not knowing.

CHORUS

Let there be rest.

Let there be peace.

Let the house breathe—

even just for a moment.

But peace is not what the gods have planned.

Chapter 4: The Gods Speak Nothing

The house is still. The pyre unlit. Herakles has returned. The family breathes again.

But the sky changes.

Not   with   thunder.

 Not with lightning.

With silence.

A silence that presses on the ears.

Then light—too sharp to be sunlight. And a figure:

IRIS enters. The gods' herald. Her voice is cold and clear.

IRIS

I do not come by choice.

But I come.

I bring another behind me.

A spirit who walks where the gods command.

CHORUS

What shadow walks behind the rainbow?

What wind curls behind the light?

Another figure follows: not fire, not storm—just presence.

LYSSA enters. She does not speak at first.

HERAKLES (confused)

What is this?

Who sent you?

I   have   returned.

 I have saved my home.

LYSSA (quietly, to Iris)

Must I?

IRIS

The order stands.

From Hera.

From the gods who will not show their faces.

LYSSA

He has suffered.

He has given everything.

Why must I be the one to break what he loves?

IRIS

You are not to question.

You are only to enter.

Lyssa pauses at the edge of the threshold.

LYSSA (to herself)

I do not hate him.

I do not wish this.

But   I   was   made   to   be   the   storm
that follows when the gods close their eyes.

She steps through the gate. Her cloak stirs no dust.
Her feet make no sound.

CHORUS

O gods—

You   do   not   lift   your   hand,
but you send her voice.

You   do   not   strike   the   blow,
but you carry the flame through another's breath.

O Herakles—

You saved the world.

But they will not save you.

Lyssa vanishes inside.

CHORUS (softly)

The house is still.

But not for long.

Chapter 5: Lyssa Enters

Inside the house, Herakles stands with his children.

He smiles. He takes off the lion skin. He leans his club against the wall.

Megara brings food. Amphitryon sits. The children laugh. The house breathes.

Then the wind changes.

Not outside.

Inside.

Herakles   pauses.

 His   smile   shifts.

 He blinks.

Once.

 Twice.

 Then not again.

He looks at his children.

But does not see them.

He steps back.

He whispers names no one knows.

He reaches for the bow.

MEGARA

Wait—what are you doing?

It's us.

Your family.

You're safe now.

But Herakles does not hear.

Not truly.

CHORUS

O   gods—

what have you done?

We see the light leave his eyes.

We   see   the   warrior   return

not   to   battle

but to a shadow the gods planted in his mind.

This is not rage.

This   is   confusion.

Disorder.

A knot unspooled.

This is Lyssa.

CHORUS

O   Herakles,

 you were our shield.

Now your hands do not know what they hold.

Your eyes do not know what they see.

And the gods?

They do not speak.

They only watch.

Chapter 6: The House Falls Without a Cry

Inside, Herakles moves.

Not with rage. Not with shouting.

With quiet confusion.

He sees monsters.

He sees threats.

He sees things that are not there.

He does not see his wife.

He does not see his sons.

He does not see his father, frozen in place.

He draws the bow.

CHORUS

Do not.

Please, do not.

But the gods have closed the sky.

And Lyssa has already left.

Herakles is alone now.

Alone with everything the gods put inside him.

 And everything they never helped him carry.

There is no scream.

No clash of sword or shield.

Only the sound of something breaking inside a man too strong to stop it.

CHORUS

O house—

You fall without fire.

You fall without stone.

You fall in silence.

We said we would watch.

We said we would stand.

But   what   do   old   men   do   when   the   strongest   hands   in   the   world   turn against themselves?

We   are   not   warriors.

We are not gods.

We are only witnesses.

And we do not look away.

Inside the house, the light fades.

There are no voices left.

Chapter 7: Theseus Comes With a Hand

The house is still.

Herakles lies in the ashes of what was once his home.

The children are gone. Megara is gone. The fire has burned nothing—but taken everything.

Herakles wakes.

Not quickly.

Not with strength.

He sits up.

He   sees   the   bow.

The   overturned   bench.

The broken stillness.

And he remembers.

"What have I done?" he asks.

"Where   is   my   family?"

"What   happened   to   my   house?"

"Was it me?"

CHORUS

Yes.

But not because you meant to.

Not because you wanted to.

Because   the   gods   gave   you   everything
 except someone to carry it with you.

HERAKLES

Let me die.

There is nothing left.

I was sent to clean the world.

And I returned to destroy the only thing that mattered.

CHORUS

There may still be one who answers.

Not in the sky.

But walking now—through the gate.

Enter THESEUS.

THESEUS

Herakles.

You do not kneel before me.

You do not end your story here.

I will take you with me.

You will not be left alone in your pain.

Not to fix you.

Not to praise you.

But to stay.

Theseus holds out his hand. Herakles takes it.

Not in joy. Not in pride. Just in need.

CHORUS

O friend who arrives not with songs,

but with silence and arms—

we see you.

You do not erase the pain.

You walk beside it.

And for that,

you are more than any god who watched.

Chapter 8: Let Us Go

The courtyard is empty.

Herakles has left with Theseus.

Amphitryon remains. Alone.

He does not speak.

He does not sit.

He stands.

At the edge of the ruined threshold.

Just as he did at the beginning.

But   now,

there   are   no   children   laughing.

No   fire   warming   the   stones.

No wife singing beneath the olive tree.

Only   him.

And the gods who stayed silent.

CHORUS

O   Thebes—

you sent no shield.

O   gods—

you watched and said nothing.

O   Herakles—

you bore too much.

O   Amphitryon—

you lost everything.

We watched.

We sang.

We did not help.

What is a chorus that cannot save?

Only   a   memory.

Only   an   echo.

Only a whisper in the ashes.

Let us go.

They turn.

They do not look back.

Discussion Questions

1. Why do the gods stay silent in this story?

    o What could they have done differently?

2. What does the chorus mean when they say "Let us go"?

    o Do you think they failed? Why or why not?

3. What did Megara do to protect her children?

    o Why did she refuse to plead with Lykos?

4. How do Theseus and Amphitryon show different ways of caring for Herakles?

    o What does it mean to "stay" even when you can't fix someone?

5. Why is there no happy ending?

    o What kind of ending does this story give instead?

Glossary

- Herakles – A Greek hero known for completing twelve impossible labors. In this story, he is broken by what the gods ask of him.

- Lyssa – A spirit of madness sent by the gods. She enters the house, not out of hate, but because she was told to.

- Amphitryon – Herakles' mortal father. He survives, but loses everything. His final silence is a moment of mourning.

- Megara – Herakles' wife. She stands between her children and death without fear or begging.

- Theseus – Herakles' friend and a ruler of Athens. He offers help when no one else will.

- Lykos – A tyrant who tries to burn the house and erase Herakles' name.

- Chorus – A group of old men who speak between scenes. They represent the city—the ones who watched, but did not act.

- Oikos – A Greek word for household, family, and everything held together by love and duty.

- Tragedy – A story where something breaks and cannot be undone. It doesn't end in rescue—but it can end in truth.

A Final Note

Sometimes we don't need a hero.

We need someone to stay.

To   stand.

 To   speak.

 To remember.

The   chorus   left.

 But you are still here.

That means the story doesn't have to end in silence.